CAPTURING CRESSELIA

Unofficial Stories
for Pokémon CoLLectors, #2

ALEX POLAN

Sky Pony Press

New York

First Edition

This is a work of fiction. Names, characters, places, and incidents are
from the author's imagination, and used fictitiously.

Sky Pony Press books may be purchased in bulk at special discounts for
sales promotion, corporate gifts, fund-raising, or educational purposes.
Special editions can also be created to specifications. For details, contact
the Special Sales Department, Sky Pony Press, 307 West 36th Street,
11th Floor, New York, NY 10018 or info@skyhorsepublishing.com.

Sky Pony® is a registered trademark of Skyhorse Publishing, Inc.®, a
Delaware corporation.

Visit our website at www.skyponypress.com.

10 9 8 7 6 5 4 3 2 1

Library of Congress Cataloging-in-Publication Data is available on file.

Special thanks to Erin L. Falligant.

Cover illustration by Matt Armstrong
Cover design by Brian Peterson

Print ISBN: 978-1-5107-1482-3
Ebook ISBN: 978-1-5107-1484-7

Printed in Canada

CHAPTER ONE

Dear Mom and Dad,

Our team challenge at Camp Pikachu this weekend is pretty fun—Pokémon Orienteering! We get to hike in the woods, canoe at the lake, and even explore a cave to find Pokémon that the counselors hid for us. We have to beat Team Fennekin if we want to make it into the Summer Camp Hall of Fame!

But . . . there's one little problem.

Tomorrow, we have to try to capture Cresselia, a Legendary Pokémon, on Crescent Isle. We get to the island by crossing the lake. On a ZIP LINE.

And, well, you know how I feel about heights.

Marco tapped his pencil against his chin, rereading what he wrote. He sighed and crossed out the last few lines. Then he wrote something else.

Tomorrow, we get to ride a ZIP LINE. Awesome! Good thing I'm not afraid of heights anymore, right? Phew!

Marco reread the letter. It sounded pretty good this time. *If only it were true,* he thought sadly. As he flipped over his pencil to erase the crossed out paragraph, he ripped a giant hole in the paper.

Great.

He crumpled up the letter just as his roommate, Logan, burst through the door of the cabin. "Let's go, buddy! Time for orienteering!"

Logan's cheeks were flushed and his sandy-brown hair messy, like usual. That's because he was always on the move. He didn't even shut the door behind him.

Marco was about to do it for him when Nisha and Maddy, the other half of Team Treecko, hurried through. Nisha tucked her lime-green T-shirt into her shorts as she eyed the notebook on Marco's desk. "Are you writing a letter for the Wingull?" she asked.

He shrugged. "I'm trying to, but . . . I mean, there's not much to write about yet. Maybe later."

Maddy cocked her blonde head like a curious puppy. "Could a Wingull really carry our letters home, like a pigeon?"

"Don't be silly. Wingulls aren't real," Nisha said gently. "It's just what our counselors call the mailbox to make letter writing more fun."

Marco hid his smile. As the youngest camper, Maddy had a *huge* imagination. Sometimes it ran away from her here at Camp Pikachu. *But so does mine,* he reminded himself, thinking about that zip line.

Every time he closed his eyes, he pictured himself on it—wobbling from a wire about a mile above the water. *Don't look down!* he'd tell himself. But he always did—just before hearing the *click* and *zip* of the harness slipping off the wire.

Marco's daydream always ended the same way—with *falling*. His stomach lurched just thinking about it.

"Are you okay?" asked Nisha, her eyes narrowed.

"Um, yeah," said Marco. "Too many pancakes this morning, I think."

She patted her own stomach. "Yeah, me, too."

That's when Marco noticed the gloves on her hands. *Gloves? In the middle of summer?* Before he could ask about them, Logan popped up in the middle of the group holding a shiny red camera.

"Say cheese! I mean, say Treecko!"

"Logan!" laughed Nisha. "That Pokédex is for orienteering." But she squished in next to Maddy for the team photo.

"I wish it really *were* a Pokédex," Logan said, checking out the photo on the camera screen.

"But it's cool that it works underwater," Marco pointed out. He couldn't wait to take the camera to the lake.

"And it's cool that we got the *red* one, like Ash in the cartoons," Logan admitted. "Team Fennekin got stuck with boring black."

"Hey! We should call it 'Dex'!" said Maddy.

Logan's eyes lit up. "Yes! Good idea, Maddy!"

She beamed as if he'd just paid her the world's greatest compliment. As she took a step toward him, he took a bigger step away, looking like he already wished he could eat his words.

Marco chuckled. Everyone knew Maddy had a *huge* crush on Logan. He turned to Marco with wild "save me!" eyes.

Marco cleared his throat. "So, do we have everything we need for today?" he asked. "Does someone have the map?"

"Check," said Nisha, patting her pocket.

"How about the compass?"

Logan's eyebrows shot up. He dug his hand into his left pocket, and then his right. "Check!" he said, pulling out the round plastic compass.

"And I have the stopwatch," said Marco, pulling it out of his pocket. "Remember not to lose any of our orienteering tools—Professor Birch said we'll lose points if we do." As he hung the stopwatch securely on a lanyard around his neck, he asked, "Do we need anything from the Poké Mart?"

"We already went," said Maddy. "Nisha bought Repel for the woods. It stops wild Pokémon from attacking us—or something like that."

Nisha pulled the green spray can from her backpack. "In other words," she said, "it protects us from mosquitoes."

"Yeah, that's what it does," said Maddy, nodding. "And I bought Lava Cookies."

"Surprise, surprise," said Marco, grinning. Maddy had the team's biggest sweet tooth. Luckily, she was pretty good about sharing—especially with Logan. "No Poké Puffs today?" he asked, which was a fancy name for cupcakes here at Camp Pikachu.

Maddy shook her head. "Lava Cookies are easier to bring," she said. "They don't get smushed."

Marco couldn't argue with that.

As Nisha shook the can of Repel, he noticed her gloved hands again. "What's with the gloves?" he asked. "Isn't it going to be like seventy degrees today?"

Nisha just sighed and stuck her hands into the pockets of her shorts, so Maddy answered for her.

"She's trying to stop biting her nails. But it's hard because her brain doesn't work when she stops chewing her nails. And she needs her brain to come up with good inventions for us so we can win."

Nisha shot Maddy a look.

"What?" asked Maddy, spreading her arms wide. "It's true!"

Logan was all ears. "What did you invent for us this time? Something that explodes? Or flies? Or, hey, how about a robot? Please, please, please say it's a robot!" He clasped his hands in his usual dramatic way.

Nisha shook her head. "I'm not telling you until we actually need them. What if they don't work? Then you'd be disappointed!"

"They'll work," said Maddy. "Your inventions *always* work." She cupped her hand by Logan's ear and whispered, "She used 3-D glasses for one of them."

"Maddy!" Nisha scolded. "Don't give it away."

"I didn't!" said Maddy. "Just about the glasses."

Nisha sighed. "Fine," she said. "I'll show you the Night Goggles."

"Night Goggles?" Marco was curious now, too.

"Yeah, they're for Pokémon Orienteering in the cave," she explained.

When she pulled a pair of cardboard 3-D glasses from her backpack, Marco recognized them right away—from the movie they'd watched last night at the Media Center. But Nisha had clipped some sort of light to the top of the glasses.

"I put together the red and blue lenses from two pairs of 3-D glasses, and then attached this infrared LED bike light." She flipped a switch on the glasses, and the light came on.

"Cool!" said Logan. He reached for the glasses and slid them onto his nose. "Wait, I don't really see anything."

"I already told you, they're Night Goggles," said Nisha, laughing. "They don't work in a bright room, but they should work well in the cave this afternoon."

"But you only have one pair?" asked Logan. "You should make more! I think I still have my 3-D glasses from last night." He flopped onto his stomach across his bed, and his head disappeared beneath it. When he popped back up, he held a pair of cardboard glasses. "Ta-da!"

"I don't know if I have time," said Nisha, reaching for the glasses. "I'd have to make them during lunch. But I can try. Do you have yours, Marco?"

He ran a hand over his head, thinking. "Maybe in my desk." But the only thing he found there was that crumpled letter, staring him in the face. "Or maybe I threw them out." *And I might as well throw this letter out, too.*

Marco grabbed the letter and headed out the door of the cabin, stopping by a metal trash bin.

Sure enough, his yellow cardboard glasses peeked out from beneath a half-eaten sandwich and a banana peel. Marco held his nose with one hand and reached for the glasses with the other. "Do you still want them?" he asked in a nasally voice.

Nisha took the glasses between two fingers, as if she were holding a dead fish. "Thanks, I think."

Then Marco threw his crumpled letter into the bin. He wished he could tell someone—his parents, his friends, *anyone*—how freaked out he was about that zip line. *But what's the point?* he wondered. *It won't change anything. I'll still be a big scaredy cat.*

As the paper ball bounced into the trashcan, Marco caught a flicker of movement from just behind the can.

Before his eyes could focus, something *yowled* and sprang at him—a flash of yellow fur careening toward his face.

Marco shrieked, leaped backward in surprise, and stumbled, falling to the ground. As he scrambled to get back up, a yellow tom cat strutted past, flicking his crooked tail.

Logan fell into a heap of laughter. "Meowth got you good!" he said, pointing at Marco.

Again, thought Marco with a sigh. No matter how many times he ran into Meowth, the grumpy cat that lived here at Camp Pikachu, the cat always caught him off guard.

He tried to calm his racing heart with a few deep breaths. But he couldn't look at Logan, who was still laughing hysterically.

I'm a scaredy cat about the zip line, thought Marco, *and now my friends think I'm actually scared of cats, too. This is going to be a really l-o-n-g weekend.*

CHAPTER TWO

"It's a Beautifly!" shouted Maddy, chasing something down the wooded trail.

Marco raced after her. "Where?"

"Shh!" Nisha whispered as she jogged toward them. "Don't let other teams hear you!" She pulled the map out of her pocket and held it up. "Wait . . . a Beautifly? That's not even one of the Pokémon we're supposed to find!"

Maddy giggled. "I know," she said. "It's a real one! Look, Logan!" She pointed toward something just off the trail, flitting around a bush.

Logan raced around the bush for a better view. "Maddy!" he said with disappointment. "That's just a *butterfly*, not a Beautifly."

Maddy gazed at the orange monarch and shrugged. "I don't care," she said. "Beautifly is a better name."

Marco couldn't argue with that. The forest seemed full of bright, colorful Beautiflies. There were also plenty of kids running around in brightly colored T-shirts—*too* many of them. He saw boys from Team Mudkip and Team Froakie in blue, and a girl from Team Chespin in brown. And who could miss that Team Torchic kid over there in the blindingly bright yellow?

Logan must have read Marco's mind, because he nudged Marco with his elbow. "How are we supposed to find the hidden Pokémon?" he asked. "As soon as we take pictures of them, all the other teams will see them, too!"

Marco suddenly spotted something and squatted down, pulling Logan with him. "We don't have to beat *all* the teams," he whispered. "Just that one." He pointed to a fox-orange T-shirt barely visible through the bushes.

"Team Fennekin," Logan spat under his breath.

"Exactly," said Marco.

As they watched, a ginormous boy in an orange T-shirt pushed through the branches, breaking what he couldn't bend. Stella, a tall girl with sharp features and a streak of magenta in her blonde hair, stepped through after him. Instead of holding the branches for her other teammates, she let them go. The branches sprang backward. "Ouch!" her red-headed brother cried. "You did that on purpose, Stella."

She probably did, thought Marco. Led by nasty Stella and her brother, Sam, Team Fennekin had been making trouble for Team Treecko since the start of camp. Now the two teams were neck and neck in the Summer Camp Hall of Fame competition. "We're going to win the Poké Ball statue," Marco whispered to Logan. "We've got this, right?"

"Right!" Logan shouted, pumping his fist in the air. With a burst of energy, he sprang up and raced past Maddy, who was nibbling on a Lava Cookie. Then he ducked his head, as if dodging something in the trail.

"Oh, no!" Logan shrieked playfully. "Maddy, it's a Beedrill!" He pointed at the bumblebee hovering over her cookie. He waved his arms wildly near the bee and then pretended to stagger backward into the grass.

Maddy didn't seem scared at all—at least not for herself. She sucked in her breath and searched for the bee. "Don't squish it!"

He didn't hear her. He was too busy hamming it up. "Run!" he shouted at Marco. "Beedrill attack! Run for your lives!" He sprinted around a bend in the trail and ran smack into a camp counselor— the one they called Professor Birch.

"Logan!" cried the counselor, his chubby cheeks flushed and his pen dangling off the clipboard. "What is it?" His shirt had come untucked from his khaki shorts, and he looked utterly confused.

Logan stood to attention. "Um, just having fun, sir. Nothing to see here."

But every kid in the clearing must have thought there *was* something to see, because they stopped to watch. Marco saw Stella smirking from the bushes. *She probably loves seeing Team Treecko getting into trouble*, he thought, clenching his jaw.

Professor Birch opened his mouth for a long moment and then shut it. He ran his hand over his goatee before saying, "Let's take it down a notch, Logan. The best trainers sneak up on Pokémon— they don't scare them all away."

Logan lowered his eyes. "Yes, sir." But as soon as Professor Birch had passed, the spring in Logan's step returned.

Marco waved Team Treecko together, trying to ignore the kids who were still staring. "Let's look at the map and make a plan, before we run out of time!" he whispered.

"Yeah, Logan," said Maddy. "Be serious. We've already wasted like"—she leaned in to look at Marco's stopwatch—"six minutes."

Logan gave an exaggerated sigh. He pretended to wipe the smirk off his face with his hand and stuff it into his pocket.

Then everyone turned to Marco, as they always did. Somehow, he'd become their fearless leader. *If only they knew that I'm* not *so fearless,* he thought sadly. But he didn't have time right now to feel sorry for himself. "Let's look at the map," he said again. "We have to know what we're looking for."

Nisha held the map steady in the center of the circle. "We're here," she said, pointing to the thick black line that marked the main trail. "And we have to find four Pokémon in an hour—less than an hour, now. See them? Bunnelby, Fletchling, Bulbasaur, and Charmander."

The Pokémon were spread throughout the forest—tiny images hidden within patches of color. "Light and dark green patches mean bushes and trees, remember?" said Nisha. "Yellow means a clearing. There are brown hills and ditches. These black blobs are rocks, and the blue on the edge of the map is the lake."

Marco studied the map and then glanced up at the woods. "Everyone is heading down the trail toward Bulbasaur," he said. "He's the closest Pokémon. But what if we split up? We have a better chance of finding more Pokémon that way."

Nisha tried to chew on her fingernail, but spat out a piece of fuzz from her glove instead. "But there's only one map and compass. How can we split those up?" Then she eyed a flat rock just off the trail and waved her friends over. "Marco, set your compass on the map," she said.

As Marco did, the red arrow bobbed toward the "N" on the dial. He watched Nisha spin the map beneath the compass until the red arrow pointed north on the map, too.

"Okay," she said. "So Bunnelby is almost straight north. We'll take the compass and follow it north. You take the map and follow the trail," she said, pointing at the dotted line.

But something niggled at Marco. "Wait," he said. "There's only one camera. How do we let each other know if we find something?"

"I know!" said Logan, raising his hand as if he were sitting in a classroom. "We'll whistle." He pursed his lips together and whistled two notes, and then repeated them.

"Hey!" said Marco. "That sounds like 'Treecko, Treecko!'"

Logan grinned and pointed to Marco. "You, sir, win the prize!"

"No fair! I can't whistle!" Maddy protested.

"That's okay," said Nisha. "You'll be with me, so I'll whistle for you."

Maddy didn't seem so sure about that. She glanced hopefully at Logan. "Or . . . Logan and I could be partners?"

Logan pretended not to hear. He was gone in a flash, already jogging down the trail. "Let's go, Marco," he called over his shoulder.

"Wait! Don't forget the hidden item," said Nisha. She showed Marco the box in the corner of the map. "If you find any mushrooms—real ones—take a picture. We can get an extra point."

Marco nodded and then raced after Logan, hoping to see his lime-green T-shirt just up ahead. He rounded a bend, and then another, breathing hard.

The crowd of kids had thinned out now, and he heard nothing but bird whistles, rustling leaves, and his own footsteps on the dirt trail. *Where's Logan?* he thought with alarm.

Then he found him—nearly tripped over him, actually.

Logan was crouched down behind a log. He pressed his finger to his lips.

So Marco squatted too, and followed Logan's gaze. A few yards away, Team Fennekin stood in front of a wooden sign. A red and white Poké Ball dangled from the post.

Bulbasaur! Marco realized.

Stella pulled out her camera while the brunette girl, Claire, studied the map. Sam stood on tiptoe, trying to see the dinosaur-like Pokémon on the wooden sign. But his huge teammate—the other boy in orange—blocked his view.

"Move over, Max!" Sam whined. "I can't see!" With his spiky red hair and freckles, he looked nothing like his sister, Stella. *He's nicer than her, too,* Marco thought. *At least, sometimes.*

"Don't be such a baby, Sam," Stella scolded. "*You* move out of the way so we can be the first team to get a picture."

"Not gonna happen," Marco heard Logan whisper, right before he shot out from behind the log and raced toward the sign. He waved one arm like a crazy person, hollering while he ran. Marco caught sight of the red camera in Logan's other hand.

Stella shrieked and stepped backward, giving Logan a clear shot at the signpost.

"Say Treecko!" he said, raising the camera and snapping a shot. Then, without missing a beat, he spun around and raced back toward Marco. Except now Stella and the big kid named Max were hot on his heels. "Run!" Logan shouted as he sprinted past.

Marco didn't have to be told twice. Stella could run—*really* run. She pointed her finger at Logan, sharp as a Beedrill's stinger.

And Max was just behind her, his bulging eyes fixed on Marco.

So Marco did the only thing he could think of. He turned and ran for his life.

CHAPTER THREE

Marco pushed through the bushes, feeling the slap and sting of a branch scraping against his cheek. He was sucking in gulps of air now, but he didn't stop. The *crunch* of brush behind him said that someone was still on his tail. Was it super-fast Stella? Or Max, who could squish him like a bug?

Don't look, Marco told himself. *Keep running!*

He took a few more steps, slipping in the muddy earth—until something grabbed him from behind.

Marco strained to break free, but someone was gripping his shirt. His feet spun in the mud.

One more yank from behind pulled him tumbling backward into the bushes.

"Hey!" Marco whirled around to face the enemy head-on. But it wasn't Team Fennekin looming over him. It was Logan, grinning like a geek.

"Stop running!" said Logan, laughing. "She's gone already. We made it." He pumped the camera in the air like a trophy.

"Really?" said Marco, trying to catch his breath. "You couldn't have just told me that?" He wiped the mud off the back of his shorts.

Logan suddenly hopped onto a rock, whistling into the air like a lonely bird. *Treecko, Treecko.*

Oh! He's signaling the girls, Marco realized. He cocked his head, listening for a response in the silent woods.

Nothing.

Logan tried again, louder this time. *Treecko, Treecko.*

Marco held his breath and strained his ears. The faintest birdcall bounced back to them. "There!" he whispered. "Did you hear it?"

Logan nodded and began jogging toward the sound, jutting off onto a narrow trail that led deeper into the woods. Every few feet, he'd whistle again. *Treecko, Treecko! Treecko, Treecko!*

The responses got louder, too. And then there they were! Nisha and Maddy appeared on the trail ahead.

"Did you find Bulbasaur?" called Nisha.

"Yes!" said Logan. "We got a great picture." He turned to Marco for a high-five.

"But I wanted to see Bulbasaur, too!" Maddy protested.

Logan handed her the camera. "Here, hold Dex. You can see Bulbasaur on there."

As she studied the photo of the green, dinosaur-like Pokémon, Maddy giggled. "You got that big Fennekin kid in this picture, too," she said. "He looks funny!"

"Let me see." Marco reached for the camera and chuckled. Max's surprised face was round and red, his mouth wide open—wide enough for a Beautifly to flutter into. He looked a lot less scary now than he had just a few minutes ago.

"We should get extra points for that," joked Logan.

"We should," said Marco, grinning. "But we probably won't." He checked his stopwatch. "Only forty-two minutes left—we have to keep hunting. Did you find Bunnelby?"

"Yes!" sang Maddy. "He was at our secret base. But we have to go back and get a picture. C'mon!"

She started half running, half skipping back up the trail.

Every team had a secret base in the woods, but Marco thought Team Treecko had the coolest one—a tree house with a ladder and a deck. A few minutes later, it came into view: as tall and strong as the Fortree City tree houses in the Pokémon video game.

The boards of the tree house were a deep chocolate brown. As Marco started to climb the ladder, the wooden rungs felt warm and welcoming in the mid-morning sun.

"It's not up there," Maddy called from beneath the tree house. "It's down here!"

Marco scrambled down as quickly as he could. A wooden sign stuck out of the earth just below the tree house. Sure enough, a rabbit-like Pokémon with enormous ears stared out from a poster tacked to the sign.

"Do you want to do the honors?" asked Logan, handing Maddy the camera.

"Yes!" She jumped in the air, looking like a rabbit herself. After snapping the picture, she stared at the screen. "I wish I had a pet rabbit," she said wistfully.

Nisha swatted at a mosquito. "But you already have a pet mouse!" she said as she pulled the Repel spray out of her backpack.

"I know," said Maddy. "But Dedenne needs a friend! I think he's lonely, especially when I'm out here orienting."

"*Orienteering,*" Nisha corrected her. "And the sooner we find those last two Pokémon, the sooner you can get back to little Dedenne."

"We need to find two Pokémon *and* a mushroom," said Maddy, correcting Nisha right back.

"Right." Nisha quickly pulled out her map, and they all huddled around her. "I think we should find Charmander next."

As Marco followed Nisha's finger across the map, his heart sank. The orange Pokémon with the flaming tail was hidden near a cluster of what looked like black rocks.

"That's right by Team Fennekin's secret base!" said Logan. "That's their cave!" He glanced excitedly at Marco, as if hoping for a prize for figuring it out.

But Marco had beaten him to the punch. And all he could think was, *What if Team Fennekin is waiting for us there?* He had outrun Stella and Max once today. He wasn't sure he could do it again.

"Race you to the cave!" said Logan, barreling past.

As Nisha and Maddy hurried after Logan, Marco sighed. He kicked at a stone in the path and then checked his stopwatch. Only twenty-nine minutes left! He dropped the timer and jogged after his team. What else could he do?

"Slow down! The cave's right there," said Marco, recognizing the rocks outside the secret fort. He spoke in a hushed voice, in case Team Fennekin was actually inside.

Every time he came near this cave, it gave him the willies. Maybe it was because last week, he'd been bombed with water balloons here during a team challenge. Marco shivered, remembering the chill of his soaking wet clothes as he ran away in defeat.

Logan, on the other hand, looked like he could hardly wait to get inside. "Should we see if Charmander is in there?" he whispered.

Marco nodded. "Go ahead," he said, his voice cracking.

"Wait, should we play Rock, Fire, Grass to see who goes in?" asked Nisha. Rock, Fire, Grass was the Pokémon version of Rock, Paper, Scissors. Team Treecko had made it up just last week.

"No, Logan can go if he really wants to," said Marco brightly, as if offering Logan the chance of a lifetime.

And Logan took him right up on it. He snuck toward the cave, ducking below the "window"—a hole in the rocky wall. He tiptoed toward the entrance and peered around the rocks into the darkness.

But as he braced himself against the rocks, he suddenly jerked his hand away. As he dove toward the ground with a shriek, a winged creature fluttered and swooped over his head.

CHAPTER FOUR

Logan rolled over, his mouth hanging open and his eyes wide.

"Did it bite you?" asked Maddy, rushing to his side.

Marco tried to run to Logan, too, but his legs were frozen. *Did I just send my friend into a cave to get attacked by a bat?*

He was relieved when Logan suddenly burst out laughing. *He never lets anything get to him for long,* thought Marco, wishing he could laugh off his fears as easily.

As Maddy sat beside Logan, patting his leg, his laughter turned into hiccups. He rolled to his knees and held up a hand. "I'm g-good," he said to Maddy. "R-really. I mean except for these annoying h-hiccups."

"Okay," said Maddy sweetly. But instead of getting off the ground, she leaned forward and peered into the cave. "Hey. . . ." she whispered. "Look what I found!"

Everyone craned their necks to see inside the cave. As Marco's eyes adjusted, he spotted it, too. Charmander grinned at them from a wooden signpost.

"Good job spotting that, Maddy!" said Nisha.

"Hey, what about me?" joked Logan. "Didn't I do a good job wiping out right in front of Charmander?"

Marco patted Logan's back. "Yeah, good job, buddy." But he felt another twinge of guilt. *If not for me, you wouldn't have wiped out in the first place. Or nearly gotten bitten by a bat!*

As Logan snapped a picture of Charmander, Nisha and Maddy studied the map, looking for the last Pokémon.

"Fletchling is by the lake," Nisha announced. "This way. C'mon!"

Marco hurried after them, trying to shake off his guilt and focus on the competition. *We have a good chance of winning this thing,* he thought—especially when Logan nearly tripped over the "hidden item" growing on a tree stump near the path.

"Mushrooms!" said Maddy. "Oh, you look just like little Shroomish." She talked to the mushrooms as if they were tiny pets she could take home with her.

"You'd better hope they're not Shroomish," said Nisha. "They release toxic spores when they're scared, and I'm pretty sure that when Logan nearly trampled them, it gave them a good scare."

"That scared *me,*" said Logan. "I think I released some toxic spores, too. Everybody run!"

Nobody ran, but everybody laughed. After getting a picture of the "Shroomish," they hurried on down the path.

Marco glanced upside down at the stopwatch dangling from his neck. "Eleven minutes!" he announced. "We have to hurry!"

"It's not far now!" called Nisha, who was in the lead. "It's by the zip line!"

Her words jolted Marco like an electric shock. As the trees thinned out, he could see it. The wooden zip line tower loomed at the water's edge—a tall platform with a zigzagging staircase that led up, up, up.

As Marco searched for the top, his stomach dropped and he stopped running.

"Are you coming?" Nisha called to him. But he couldn't speak. It felt like he had a lump in his throat the size of a Shroomish.

Think of something funny! he told himself. *Make a joke, like Logan would.*

But he couldn't think either—his mind went blank.

"Let's go!" shouted Logan, racing toward the stairs. "I'll bet Fletchling is hidden at the top!" But a hanging sign at the base of the stairs stopped him in his tracks.

"Aw, man," he called back to his friends. "We're not supposed to climb on it yet."

Marco felt a wave of relief, but Logan wouldn't stop talking about the zip line. "It'll feel like flying on Latios, the dragon Pokémon in the video game," he said excitedly. "Soaring faster than a jet plane over the water. I can't wait!"

"Me neither," agreed Nisha. "It's probably the coolest thing we've done here at Camp Pikachu. I wish I'd invented it!" She quickly studied the ropes and pulleys stretching toward the little island.

At least my teammates are excited about it, Marco told himself. *So if I'm a big baby and chicken out, there'll be* someone *from Team Treecko to cross over.*

That thought made him feel slightly better, but he still couldn't look at the zip line. He looked past it, above it, and around it, finally zeroing in on his stopwatch. "We have to go," he said, lifting the timer so others could see. "Only six minutes left. Fletchling isn't here. The sign must be farther down by the pier!"

His teammates followed him, like they always did. But as he ran, he felt less sure of himself with every step. He hadn't even looked at the map. Where exactly was he going?

Just keep running, he told himself. *The farther away from the zip line, the better.*

But as Marco and his friends searched the tall grass near the lakeshore, time ticked away—faster than quicksand. Five minutes. Three minutes. One minute. Every time he checked the stopwatch, they were getting nearer and nearer to. . . .

Thweet! Professor Birch's whistle cut through the air.

"Game over," said Nisha sadly. "At least this part of it."

"Fletchling must be here *somewhere*, though," said Marco, still searching. "Keep looking!"

"Yeah, don't stop!" shouted Logan, who was crouched down inspecting a hollowed-out log.

Then Marco heard a cheer erupt from behind him. *Yes!* "Who found it?" he asked, whirling around to see if it was Nisha or Maddy.

But the cheer hadn't come from one of the girls. It hadn't come from Team Treecko at all.

A cluster of kids in bright yellow tees were racing away from the zip line toward Team Treecko. *They found Fletchling!* thought Marco. He was sure of it. *They found Fletchling right where my teammates were looking—before I told them the Pokémon wasn't there.*

As Team Torchic passed by, triumphant smiles on their faces, Marco caught Logan's eye.

"Let's go!" mouthed Logan. He raced back toward the zip line.

"But the whistle blew!" Maddy protested.

Marco ignored her—and shrugged Nisha's hand off his arm. He had to get back to the zip line to find Fletchling, before it was too late.

As they neared the wooden tower, Marco scanned it for any sign of the red bird-like Pokémon. "There!" he shouted to Logan. "Is that a Poké Ball?" Something dangled just below the bottom platform of the tower.

But before he could check it out, another *thweet!* cut through the air. And Officer Jenny stepped from the woods, blocking Marco's path. She was the sternest counselor at camp. And when she saw which direction the boys were running in, her eyes narrowed.

"Time's up," she said firmly, holding her hand like a stop sign. "You know the rules, boys. If you keep searching after the whistle, you *lose* points instead of gaining them."

Marco's legs wobbled like wet noodles beneath him. *I blew it with Fletchling,* he thought, fighting back hot tears. *Did I just get my team in trouble, too?*

CHAPTER FIVE

As Marco walked toward the Dining Hall, he held his breath. He couldn't even bring himself to glance at Logan, who trudged along beside him. Officer Jenny walked a few feet behind, not saying a word.

The stony silence was almost unbearable. *Is she going to punish us?* wondered Marco. *I wish she'd just do it already!*

But she didn't. When they reached the entrance to the Dining Hall, Officer Jenny put a hand on each boy's shoulder and leaned over to say just five words. "Don't let that happen again."

"Yes, ma'am," whispered Marco. But as soon as she was gone, he exhaled loudly, dropping onto the bench of a picnic table.

"That was a close one," said Logan, his face pale.

"Too close," said Marco. "We almost lost points. I don't even think I can eat now."

"Me, neither," said Nisha. "Besides, there's no time—I have to go make that second pair of Night Goggles. See you at the lake!" She was gone in a flash, before Marco could even apologize.

But Maddy was still there. "I *told* you guys about the whistle," she said, her hands on her hips.

"I know," said Marco sadly. "I'm sorry—we should have listened to you."

When Logan finally apologized, too, Maddy perked back up. "It's pizza day! Let's get in line."

Marco shook his head. "I'm not hungry. I'll just meet you at the lake." What he really wanted to do was go back to his cabin and crawl under the covers. *But in half an hour, we have to start orienteering all over again,* he reminded himself. *Ready or not.*

Maddy sat on the side of the pier, swinging her legs above the water. "I get seasick," she said again. "I can't help it. So I'm just going to stay here."

Logan groaned. "You couldn't have told us about this seasickness stuff earlier?" he asked, buckling his life vest. "Maybe Nurse Joy could have given you some medicine or something."

Maddy shrugged. "I didn't know it would be so wavy!" she said, pointing at the wind rippling across the water.

Marco could tell her mind was made up. Maddy was as stubborn as any of them—sometimes more. *Will I be that strong if I have to tell my teammates that I can't do the zip line?* he wondered. He hoped so, but his palms got sweaty just thinking about it.

"It's okay," Nisha told Maddy. "The three of us can go out in a canoe, and you can stay on the pier. But first, you should try out my new invention!" She pulled something from her backpack that looked like a snorkel.

Maddy shrunk backward. "I don't . . . really like to snorkel," she said.

"It's not a snorkel," said Nisha. "It's a Snorkel *Stick*—like a Selfie Stick. You put the camera on it so you can take video underwater! I'll show you how it works."

Logan handed her the camera, and she screwed it onto a piece of black plastic attached to the Snorkel Stick.

"Is that part of a tripod?" Marco asked, pointing to the black thing.

"Yup," said Nisha. "From home. I knew it would come in handy." Then she handed the Snorkel Stick to Maddy. "I set up the camera to take a video, so you can dunk it under the water. But be careful. Don't let go!"

"I won't," Maddy promised. She carefully stretched out on her stomach, holding the purple stick. Then she lowered the camera over the edge of the pier. "Like this?" she asked.

"Yes," said Nisha. "Spin it in a slow circle so you get a video of everything that's under there."

Maddy did, sticking her tongue out in concentration as she slowly spun the stick.

Marco wondered what she'd find under the water, but he could almost hear the ticking of the stopwatch around his neck. Most of the other teams were already by the boathouse, where Officer Jenny was helping them get into canoes.

"We ran out of time in the woods," Marco reminded his friends. "We need to go get our canoe!"

"Okay, Maddy, bring it back up," said Nisha.

When Maddy did, Nisha unscrewed the camera from the Snorkel Stick and replayed the video. Marco watched the screen out of the corner of his eye, keeping the other eye on the canoes that were starting to drift past.

The video didn't show much. Something that looked like seaweed swirled round and round in the green water near the posts of the pier. Then Marco spotted a flash of color—something red and white.

"Wait, was that a Poké Ball?" Logan asked. "Go back!"

"It could have been a fishing bobber," said Marco.

"It wasn't," said Logan. "It was a Poké Ball. I'll bet it's on the other side of the pier!" He flopped onto his stomach and stuck his head below the pier, as if he were looking under his bed again.

"Here it is! Come see!"

Just below Logan, tacked to the wooden pier, was a laminated poster of a Pokémon. And below that, a half-submerged Poké Ball bobbed in the water.

Nisha handed Logan the camera so he could snap a photo, upside-down.

"Horsea!" Maddy cried when she saw the picture, which looked like a tiny blue seahorse. "We found Horsea!"

"Shh! Not so loud!" Nisha whispered.

But it was too late.

A taunting voice rang out across the water. "Whatcha got there?"

Stella drifted toward them in her canoe, perched like a queen on her throne. Claire sat in front, but she glanced away as soon as Marco met her eyes.

"Looks like you found Horsea," said Stella, gesturing toward the poster that Logan didn't have time to hide. "And now I did, too." She raised her camera and snapped a picture.

"See ya later, losers," she sneered as the canoe pulled away. Marco heard her barking orders to Claire, who seemed to be doing all the paddling.

"What a cheater!" cried Logan, his hands balled into fists.

Marco almost reminded him that they had done the same thing to Team Fennekin, back in the woods. But Logan was already racing down the pier toward shore. "Let's get her!" he cried.

Marco ran after Logan, feeling the pier wobble beneath him with each step. Then he was on dry ground, hurrying toward an empty canoe.

Officer Jenny, wearing a blue life vest over her swimsuit and a sun visor instead of her usual police cap, lifted one end of the aluminum canoe and dragged it toward the water. "Where's the last member of your team?" she asked.

"Maddy's not coming. She gets seasick," Nisha explained in one winded breath.

Marco glanced over his shoulder and saw that Maddy had flopped back down onto the pier, looking like a melted Poké Puff left out in the rain. He sighed, knowing just how she felt.

"I see," said Officer Jenny. "Well, this canoe is big enough for the three of you. Just don't stand up or rock the boat. And don't make Professor Birch blow his whistle." She gestured toward the lifeguard chair.

"We . . . won't," said Marco, his voice cracking. He'd had enough whistle-blowing for one day.

"But there are only two seats!" Logan noticed as he carefully stepped into the boat.

"You and Nisha can have them," Marco said quickly. "I'll sit in the middle." *So I don't have to paddle,* he thought. Because after what had happened in the woods, he didn't want to be in charge anymore. *We'll be better off with someone else leading the way.*

"You'll be on map duty then," said Nisha, handing him the new orienteering map. This one was mostly blue, with an outline of greens, blacks, and browns.

Then Officer Jenny helped them push off from shore. Logan sat at the rear of the boat, which meant he got to steer. Nisha took the front. And Marco hung out in the middle, trying to use his map and compass to steer the team toward another Pokémon. *So much for not leading the way,* he thought with a sigh.

"Where's Stella?" asked Logan from behind. "Oh, I see her! Let's go." He began paddling furiously toward a canoe in the distance.

"No!" Nisha scolded, dragging her paddle in the water like a brake. "We're supposed to hunt for Pokémon—not Team Fennekin. Where should we go, Marco?"

He studied the map, looking for Pokémon. Wingull was hidden somewhere in the grass near shore. Goldeen was back toward the boathouse. And Tentacool was. . . .

A *whoop* from the swimming raft in the middle of the lake told him *exactly* where Tentacool was.

"That way!" Logan shouted, pointing toward the cluster of Team Froakie T-shirts surrounding the raft. He switched his paddle to the left side of the boat, sending a trickle of cold water down Marco's back.

Marco yelped and scooted up onto his knees.

"Don't stand up!" Nisha warned over her shoulder. "You heard what Officer Jenny said."

"Okay, okay," he said, wiping the water from the back of his neck. "Look for a Pokémon that looks like a blue jellyfish!" he reminded his friends.

"There!" cried Nisha, pointing with her paddle.

A poster of Tentacool was tacked to the side of the raft, rippling in the wind. "Quick, get a picture!" said Marco.

Logan fished the camera out of his pocket and leaned over the side of the canoe, making it tip toward the water.

"Don't rock the boat!" Nisha shrieked, gripping the sides of the boat with her hands. "You're making me nervous."

Then Marco saw something that made *him* nervous: two girls in fox-orange T-shirts paddling straight toward the canoe.

Logan saw them, too. "No way," he said. "Team Fennekin's not getting a picture of *this* Pokémon."

As soon as Stella and Claire were closer—close enough for Marco to see the sneer on Stella's face—Logan launched into action. He paddled the canoe forward a few feet, right in between Stella's canoe and the Tentacool poster.

Then he pointed at Claire. "Don't look now," he called in a panicked voice, "but Tentacool's in your boat! He's alive! Get out! Get out!"

Claire jumped and spun around in the boat, which made Stella snort.

"You fell for that?" she said, giving Claire a withering look. Then she reached her hand over the side of the boat and scooped up some water, preparing to attack Logan.

"Stella, get your hand out of the water—NOW!" he cried. "There's a fin. Look! There it is! Shark! It's Sharpedo!"

He stood up and pointed at the rippling water near Stella's hand.

"Don't. Stand. Up!" Nisha cried.

Too late.

Marco felt the boat flip. For a moment, he hung suspended in the air—as if his harness had just broken away from a zip line, and he was about to fall down, down, down. . . .

He hit the water with a sharp *slap*.

And then he couldn't breathe.

CHAPTER SIX

As Marco plunged into the icy cold water, his lungs tightened and the world went black.

He went under for just a second before his life vest popped him back up again. But now his arms and legs felt frozen—stiff with cold and fear. *Swim!* he told himself. But where was the boat? Where was Logan? Where was Nisha?

Marco faced shore, where Maddy stood on the pier with her hands clamped over her mouth.

He saw Professor Birch leap out of the lifeguard chair and race toward the boathouse. And then he spotted Officer Jenny paddling toward him and the overturned canoe.

Someone sputtered behind Marco. "Logan!"

His friend looked like a drowned rat, his wet bangs pressed to his forehead. Logan opened his mouth, as if to crack a joke, and then closed it again.

"Where's N-Nisha?" asked Marco, his teeth starting to chatter.

"Here!" she called. She was clinging to the overturned canoe on the other side of the swim raft.

Everyone's okay, Marco realized with relief.

But then he caught sight of another canoe— and Stella's smug face. She didn't say a word.

She doesn't have to, thought Marco miserably, turning back toward shore.

"I'm sorry," Logan said again. "I was just trying to scare Team Fennekin." Instead of looking at his teammates, he studied Dex, which luckily had been strapped to his wrist during the fall.

"How'd that work out for you?" asked Nisha, her tone sharp. She hugged her towel tightly around her shoulders.

Marco felt like a referee at a boxing match. Logan and Nisha had been going at it ever since

Officer Jenny had brought them back to the pier to dry out. At least their bickering took Marco's mind off the tipped canoe.

After falling into the lake, all he could think about was the zip line tomorrow. *I fell out of the canoe. Am I going to fall off the zip line, too?* Now the danger seemed more real than ever.

As Marco wrung out his T-shirt over the edge of the pier, he spotted Maddy playing peacekeeper with Logan and Nisha.

"Do you want to share this with Nisha?" she asked Logan as she broke a soft Lava Cookie in half.

"Not now," he grumbled. "We have to look for more Pokémon."

"Yeah, we do," said Marco, checking his stopwatch. He was relieved that it still worked, even dripping wet. "We already lost half an hour." Then, out of the corner of his eye, he spotted a canoe approaching the pier.

"Incoming," said Logan under his breath.

Red-headed Sam was at the front of the boat, waving to make sure he had their attention. Then he made goofy swimming motions with his hands. "Did you have a nice swim?" he teased.

"Yeah, how's the water, Team Treecko?" called Max from the rear of the canoe.

As the boys paddled away, Nisha groaned and stood up. Water dribbled from her khaki shorts, and her shoes squeaked. As she peeled off her wet gloves and shoved them into her pockets, she asked, "Where's the map, Marco? Let's get going."

The map? He checked his pockets, but he already knew they were empty. He'd been clutching the compass in his hand ever since the boat tipped into the lake, but what had he done with the map?

"It was . . . on my lap," he mumbled. "Before, you know, the boat tipped." He raised his eyes to meet Nisha's, and then they both shifted their gaze toward the lake.

"Is it out there?" asked Logan, getting to his feet. "Do you see it?"

After a long painful pause, Marco said, "No. And even if I did, it'd be ruined by now." *Ruined, like everything else I try to do during orienteering.*

"Well do you at least remember what was on it?" asked Nisha. "What are the last two Pokémon we're looking for?"

Marco closed his eyes and tried to remember. "Wingull was somewhere on shore"—he gestured toward the beach and swimming area—"and Goldeen was in the water on the other side of the boathouse. But without the map. . . ."

"It doesn't matter," said Nisha, waving her hand in the air. "What was the hidden item? Let's make sure to get a picture of that."

Marco sunk back down again. "I don't know," he said. "I didn't see it on the map—or I just can't remember." He pressed his fingertips against his forehead.

A heavy silence fell over the pier, which Maddy tried to break. "Lava Cookie?" she asked, holding the treat below Marco's nose.

The sweet smell almost made him gag. "No, thanks," he said quickly.

Maddy's face fell, and she started crumbling bits of cookie into the water below. "I'm sorry I'm not helping," she said sadly.

Nisha leaned over to squeeze her shoulder. "C'mon, you can help right now. We'll search the beach for Wingull while the boys look for Goldeen in the water."

Maddy smiled and hopped up, taking Nisha's hand.

Marco emptied the water from his shoes before heading back to the boathouse with Logan.

A lost map. A flipped canoe. What next? he thought as he walked. He shivered, partly from his drenched clothes, and partly from his fear that something else could go wrong. Something else *would* go wrong. By now, he was almost certain of it.

"We should give Stella a taste of her own medicine," said Logan, paddling with short, quick strokes. "We should spy on Team Fennekin until they find Goldeen!"

Marco shaded his eyes from the sun and searched the lake for Team Fennekin. "That plan's not going to work," he said with a sigh. "I think Team Fennekin already found all the Pokémon."

He pointed toward the boathouse they had just left behind, where Stella and Claire were stepping out of their canoe. Stella was doing some sort of weird victory dance. And Team Torchic wasn't far behind. Two kids in bright yellow tees were dragging their canoe out of the water, too.

"I can't look," Logan groaned, burying his face in his hands. "I can't stand it. Just kill me now."

Marco wanted to give up, too. The sun had suddenly gone behind a cloud and refused to come back out.

Then they heard it—a whistle from the beach. *Treecko, Treecko!*

"The girls!" said Marco. "They must have found Wingull!"

He and Logan paddled toward the sandy shore, where Nisha was waving. She helped them pull the canoe onto the beach.

"You found Wingull?" asked Logan, hopping out of the boat. "Let me see."

Maddy popped up out of some tall grass beyond the beach. She raised a finger to her lips and waved them over, as if warning them not to wake a sleeping baby.

When Marco saw the poster of the seagull-like Pokémon, he had to look away. Seeing Wingull only reminded him of the letter he'd written to his parents. *The letter I never sent, because I chickened out,* he thought sadly.

"You couldn't find Goldeen?" asked Nisha.

Logan shook his head. "Not yet. I don't think Goldeen is even out there. I think the counselors tricked us," he said, kicking the sand.

"But Team Fennekin found it," Marco pointed out. When Logan shot him an annoyed look, he wished he'd kept his mouth shut.

Nisha sighed. "How much time do we have?" she asked.

Marco checked his stopwatch. "Seven min-utes?!" he cried. "When did that happen?" He shook the timer, not convinced it was working.

"We have to keep looking!" said Logan, rush-ing back to the canoe.

Marco ran, too, but a wave of hopelessness washed over him. He was pretty sure they weren't going to find Goldeen.

And he was right. A few minutes later when Professor Birch's whistle cut through the air, he and Logan were floating in the middle of the lake. *We lost—again,* was all he could think.

Nisha noticed Marco's long face back on shore. "Don't worry about it," she said. "We'll do better at the cave, okay?"

Marco nodded and tried to muster up some sort of energy. *We* have *to do better at the cave,* he told himself. *Because the only competition after that is the zip line, and I'm pretty sure that's going to be an epic fail.*

"Let's go!" cheered Logan. "To the cave!" He never seemed to have trouble finding energy.

Marco raced after his friend, hoping some of that energy would rub off on him. But another sharp whistle cut through the air, stopping him in his tracks.

"Team Treecko!" Officer Jenny called from behind.

Uh-oh. Marco's stomach dropped, just like it did when he and Logan had gotten busted in front of the zip line this morning. *But what did we do wrong this time?*

He couldn't bring himself to turn around.

CHAPTER SEVEN

Marco finally turned to face Officer Jenny—and was relieved to see a twinkle in the counselor's eyes.

"I know you're eager to go cave hunting," she said, "but you need to make a stop first—back at your cabins, to put on dry clothes."

"But, there's no time!" Logan protested.

"No buts," said Officer Jenny, kindly but firmly. "It's chilly in the cave. And the more time you waste arguing with me, the less time you'll have for orienteering. You can make up time riding your bikes to the cave."

Marco took a deep, ragged breath as he watched the rainbow of colored T-shirts disappear into the distance. Everyone else was heading forward toward the cave.

But us? he thought, glancing at his teammates. *It's like we're moving backward with every step we take.*

Marco pedaled as fast as he could, trying to keep up with Logan, but he kept daydreaming—his mind drifting to the zip line.

Riding bikes feels like flying. Except I'm not scared, he realized, *because I'm a whole lot closer to the ground. Why does that zip line have to be so high up, anyway?*

He thought about asking Nisha if she could rig up another zip line—one just above the water. He imagined his toes skimming the lake as he crossed to Crescent Isle. His friends would be waving to him from the island, but he wouldn't be in such a rush to get there. He'd just lean back in the harness, raise his face to the sun, and enjoy the ride. . . .

"Earth to Marco."

Logan's voice brought the zip line ride to a screeching halt. He had slowed down so that Marco could catch up with him.

"Yeah?"

"What's the matter? Are you wishing you had a bike like mine?" asked Logan.

Marco glanced at his friend's bike. "Our bikes are *exactly* the same." Everyone had rented bikes from the Rydel's Cycles stand behind the Poké Mart. They were all blue. All shiny. All new.

"Actually," Logan insisted, "mine's an Acro Bike, like in the Pokémon video game. I'll bet yours can't do this." He pulled back on the handlebars and did a wheelie—a small one, but when he brought his front tire back down, he looked pretty proud.

"Yeah, you're right," said Marco, because it was easier than arguing. "Mine can't do that." *I'll leave the wheelies to Logan,* he thought. *And the zip line, too.*

"Really? Wheelies?" said Nisha, who was riding just behind them. "After what happened with the canoe?" She still seemed pretty grumpy about that. "Maddy, hurry up!" she called over her shoulder. "Do you have your Night Goggles with you?"

"Yup," Maddy responded as she pedaled up to the rest of the group. "I can't wait to use them to find Zubat!"

"Find *who*?" asked Logan, circling back on his bike.

"Zubat!" said Maddy. "He's like a purple bat. I'm pretty sure he'll be one of the Pokémon we get to find in the cave—because bats live in caves, you know."

"Um, yeah, I know," joked Logan. He circled the group again on his bike and then said, "Luckily, I'm riding my Acro Bike, which is faster than any old Zubat. Wanna see?"

He took off on his bike—in the opposite direction.

"Logan!" cried Marco. "We're already late! What are you doing?"

"Showing you my bunny hop!" came Logan's response, muffled by the wind.

"His bunny what?" asked Maddy. She was all ears for anything that had to do with animals.

"His bunny hop. It's a bike trick," Marco explained. "You use it to hop over something." But he couldn't believe Logan was showing off his trick right *now*.

Logan turned around again and raced past them, aiming his front tire for a puddle in the road. Just before he reached it, he pulled up his handle-bars so that the tire cleared the puddle. He tried to pull up his back tire, but it crashed down into the puddle with a *splash*. When Logan circled back to the group, the backs of his legs were splotched with mud.

"Good job!" said Maddy clapping.

"I didn't actually do it," Logan grumbled. "Let me try again."

"But we're running late," said Marco. "Don't you want to get to the cave?" For some reason, Logan didn't seem all that worried about being on time for the competition.

"Just one more try," said Logan, pedaling away before anyone could talk him out of it. This time, he aimed for something in the road *behind* them.

When Marco saw what it was, he did a double take. A broken branch! "Logan, don't—!" he started to say.

But it was too late. Logan's front tire cleared the branch easily, but his back one came down way too soon. The branch cracked, twigs flew, and Logan's bike skidded off the path—taking Logan with it. He disappeared into the ditch.

CHAPTER EIGHT

Marco dropped his bike and sprinted toward the ditch. Logan hadn't screamed. Or yelled. Or laughed. Or *anything*. He was quiet—way too quiet.

"Logan!" Marco cried as he half-ran, half-tripped into the ditch.

Then he spotted him, sitting up in the grass beside his tipped bike.

Marco blew out the breath he'd been holding. "Are you okay?" He squatted in the grass beside his friend.

Logan just sat there, dabbing at the blood trickling from his elbow. Finally he turned toward

Marco, as if noticing him for the first time. "Yeah, I'm okay," he said in a tiny voice.

"Are you sure?" asked Marco. "You don't look so great."

Logan shrugged. Then he slowly pushed himself up to standing. "I'm okay." He reached for his bike.

"Do you still want to go to the cave?" asked Nisha, sounding doubtful.

"You can wear Night Goggles!" chimed in Maddy. "Nisha made two pairs." She stood close to Logan, as if she feared he'd topple over at any moment.

He smiled at Maddy's offer.

"We'll find the Pokémon for sure," said Maddy. "Especially Zubat!"

Suddenly, Logan's smile faded, and he looked down at his ankle. "Actually, my ankle is starting to hurt. I think I might have sprained it." He rolled down his sock and rubbed the spot.

"Can you walk on it?" asked Marco. "Should we take you to the Health Center?" Logan was usually so tough. *He must be really hurt,* thought Marco, wishing he knew what to do.

Logan hesitated. "I think I can ride my bike there," he said.

"Okay, I'll go with you," said Marco quickly. "And Nisha and Maddy can go to the cave."

"What? No!" said Maddy. "I'm going with Logan, too." She crossed her arms as if to say, "Don't even try to talk me out of it."

Nisha sighed. "You two take Logan to the Health Center. And I'll ride to the cave so that one of us is there when they start the orienteering. Wish me luck."

As Marco helped Logan onto his bike, he tried not to worry. But what if Logan was really hurt? What if he couldn't explore the cave?

It was only halfway through the competition, but between Maddy's seasickness and Logan's sprained ankle, it seemed the members of Team Treecko were dropping like flies.

"When do you take a Pokémon to the doctor?"

Maddy didn't answer. She just stared at Nurse Joy.

Marco stared, too. The nurse didn't have pink pigtails like Nurse Joy in the Pokémon cartoons, but when the light shone on her hair, he could see faint streaks of pink. The only thing more interesting than her hair was the clock on the wall, which *ticked* forward much too quickly. *Is Nisha exploring the cave yet?* he wondered.

"How about you?" the pretty nurse said to Logan as she examined his ankle. "Can you guess? When do you take a Pokémon to the doctor?"

"I—I don't know," said Logan, squinting into the light above the exam table.

"When its Bulb-is-sore," said the nurse, smiling. "Get it?"

Maddy giggled. "I get it. You know, Logan—Bulbasaur, like the Pokémon."

His mouth twitched a little.

"Jokes make everything hurt less, don't you think?" said the nurse. "Laughter is the best medicine."

Usually, Logan was all about jokes. But right now, he seemed so quiet. *Is his ankle hurting* that *much?* Marco wondered.

When the nurse asked Logan to move his foot up and down, he did, wincing a little.

"Hmm," she said, gently pressing against his skin. "It doesn't look bruised or swollen. Can you stand on it?"

Logan did, but when she asked him to take a few steps, he could only limp. Nurse Joy helped him back to the exam table.

"You might have a minor sprain," she said. "Let's wrap your ankle and get you an ice pack. And you should stay off it for a while."

"Wait . . . what?" said Marco, louder than he'd intended. "But we're supposed to explore the cave!" He waited for Logan to protest, too, but he didn't.

Maddy didn't seem all that impressed with the nurse's diagnosis. "Don't you have any Heal Powder?" she asked, eyeing up the glass jars and silver canisters on the nurse's shelf.

Nurse Joy smiled. "Nope, I'm fresh out of that." She started wrapping Logan's ankle with a pinkish bandage.

"Well, how about Potions?" asked Maddy. She had her hand on her hip, as if she were quizzing Nurse Joy.

The nurse shook her head. "No Potions either," she said. "However, I do have an ice pack in the freezer—and maybe a few Poké Puffs in there, too."

Marco watched Maddy's eyes light up. Nurse Joy had said the two magic words that could cure Maddy from any funk: *Poké Puffs*.

"You keep your Poké Puffs in the *freezer*?" asked Maddy.

The nurse nodded. "I like to eat mine cold," she said. "Want to see?"

Maddy nodded and followed Nurse Joy out of the room.

"Well, at least Maddy's happy now," said Marco as he sat down next to Logan. "Are you okay?"

Logan shrugged as he examined his wrapped ankle. "I guess you'll have to explore the cave without me."

Marco bit his lip. He wanted to shake Logan. *Where's my friend who always laughs things off?* he wondered. *The one who gets right back up and keeps on going?*

But he said nothing, because the truth was, he wasn't just worried about Logan. He was also worried about himself. A new fear had started to creep into his thoughts: *What if Logan has to stay off his ankle* tomorrow *too?*

When the nurse came back in with an ice pack and a pair of crutches, Marco's heart sank. Things weren't looking good.

"Hey, Marco," said Maddy, swallowing a bite of chocolate Poké Puff. "Which Pokémon always sneezes?"

"Huh?" he said, furrowing his brow.

"I'm telling a joke!" said Maddy. "Which Pokémon always sneezes? Do you know the answer or not?"

Marco shook his head.

"Pik-ACHOO!" Maddy said gleefully, laughing her head off.

Marco forced a smile. "Good one," he said. But there was something he had to ask Nurse Joy, and this was no joke. He pointed toward Logan's wrapped ankle. "How long does he have to stay off it? I mean, can he do the, um . . . the orienteering tomorrow?" He couldn't bring himself to say the words *zip line*.

Nurse Joy shook her head. "If Logan's ankle is as sore as he says it is, zip lining would be a bad idea. I'll write a note for Professor Birch excusing him from the competition, okay?"

No! Marco wanted to scream. *Not okay!*

Because there was no way he could face the zip line without Logan by his side.

No. Way.

CHAPTER NINE

When Marco's cheek started to quiver, he turned away. He didn't know if he was going to cry or totally go off on Logan for bailing on him.

He didn't actually bail on you, Marco reminded himself. *He got hurt—that's different. And Maddy and Nisha will still be there tomorrow.*

So he took a deep breath and faked his best cheerful voice. "Maddy and I had better get to the cave. Are you going to be okay, Logan?"

"I'll make sure he gets back to his cabin safely," said Nurse Joy kindly. "Maybe after a Poké Puff?"

Logan's eyes lit up, but Marco's stomach twisted at the thought of eating at a time like this. He tried to smile as he hurried out the door, practically dragging Maddy behind him.

Team Treecko—or what was left of it—made it to the cave in record time.

Marco was relieved to see Officer Jenny standing just outside the cave, which meant they hadn't totally missed orienteering today. But in her blue vest and police officer cap, she looked especially stern. She tapped her watch. "You've got twenty-five minutes left. And Nisha has your team map. See if you can find her right away."

Marco swallowed hard as he reached down to set his stopwatch. It was tough enough to find Pokémon with a full *hour*. How were they going to find any in just twenty-five minutes?

"Wow, it's dark in here," Maddy said from inside the cave. As he followed her in, he felt the temperature drop—and was almost grateful that Officer Jenny had made them change out of their wet clothes.

The cave was definitely dark. Marco could barely see his hand in front of his face. As his eyes adjusted, he heard Maddy fumbling around in her backpack.

Then, with the *click* of a switch, he was blinded all over again—this time by a bobbing bright light.

"Let me guess. Night Goggles?" he asked, shielding his face from the glare.

"Yup," said Maddy happily. "Hey, look at that staircase. It's just like Granite Cave!"

Marco couldn't see the stairs. He couldn't see anything except the shining light that Maddy had become, so he carefully followed her glow up the rock steps.

Eventually, he could see the cave walls around them. This *did* look like Granite Cave from the Hoenn region. He felt like a player in a video game!

They were entering a torch-lit cavern with lots of cracks and crevices. A team of kids explored a corner of the cave, but in the shadows, Marco couldn't tell what color their shirts were.

"Let's see if Nisha is over there," he said to Maddy.

As they got closer, Marco saw the flash of a camera. Kids laughed and scurried away from the wall, as if they'd just struck gold.

"Did they find a Pokémon?" asked Maddy as they rushed toward the wall. "Do you see it?"

"No," he answered. "Without the map, I don't even know what we're looking for!" He searched up high while Maddy got down on her hands and knees to explore the rocks down below.

"Here!" she cried. "Oh—ha! Look what the counselors did!"

Marco knelt down and spotted it, too. The poster of a rock-like Pokémon had been wrapped around a boulder to make it round and bulging, like a real Pokémon. "Is that Geodude?" he asked.

"I don't know," she said. "Nisha will know, though. She always knows."

"That's true," said Marco. "She's like a walking Pokédex. Well, let's get a picture—quick." Then it hit him like a rockslide.

We can't take a picture.

They couldn't take a picture, because they didn't have the camera. *Logan* still had the camera.

Marco sunk down on a rock and buried his face in his hands.

"What's wrong?" Maddy asked, shining her light on him as if he were a Pokémon she'd just discovered.

"Logan has the camera," he said, his voice muffled by his fingers. "And I've got the compass. And Nisha has the map. But if none of us are together, what good are all those things? We can't capture any Pokémon!"

"Oh." Maddy's voice sounded small in the darkness. "Well, we could still keep *looking* for them. I'll bet Zubat is in here somewhere. . . ."

Marco shook his head. How could Maddy be cheerful at a time like this? But when he felt her hand on his arm, his frustration started to melt away. *If Maddy's not going to quit, then I can't either.*

He stood up and brushed off the back of his shorts. "Okay, Maddy," he said. "Lead the way."

She did, right out of the cave and into a dark connecting tunnel. "So what does a Zubat look like, anyway?" he asked as they walked.

"Duh. It's a bat!" she said, giggling.

"A Zubat is a Poison- and Flying-type Pokémon, to be exact," added a deep voice.

Marco jumped about a mile high. "Who's there?" he asked, spinning in a circle.

Professor Birch stood just a few feet away, shielding his eyes from the light of the Night Goggles. "It's me," he said. "Your favorite counselor. But the real question is, what in the land of Hoenn are you wearing on your head?"

Maddy took off the Night Goggles and showed them to him while Marco tried to calm his racing heart.

"Ah, interesting," said Professor Birch. "We tried to light up most of the rooms in the cave, but these glasses will come in handy in some of the darker spots. You never know which Pokémon might be hiding there." He winked at Maddy as he handed back her Night Goggles.

"We don't even know which Pokémon to look for," Maddy confessed, "because we don't have the map—Nisha does."

"Or a camera," Marco added bleakly. He explained what had happened to Logan's ankle.

Professor Birch stroked his goatee thoughtfully. "Well, I'm sure we can find a solution," he said. "Keep searching for Nisha, and if your team can show me where you found the Pokémon, I'll make sure you get the points for them."

Maddy bounced forward and gave the counselor a quick hug. Marco felt like hugging him, too, but tried to control himself.

"Alright now, you don't have much time," said Professor Birch, holding up his hand to block any future hugs. "Get going, and remember to keep an eye out for glittery rocks." He stepped aside so that they could pass by.

"Glittery rocks must be the hidden item," Maddy whispered. "He gave us a clue!"

"Yup," said Marco. "But he also said that we don't have much time. C'mon!"

He could already hear voices from the end of the tunnel, which opened into another cavernous room. Kids were scattered around, poking their heads into tunnels that led from the cave to who knows where.

"Wow," said Maddy, taking it all in. "Do you see Nisha?"

"No," said Marco, but he wasn't really looking for her—because his eyes had spotted artwork on the walls. "Check it out," he said. "This really *is* like Granite Cave!"

Above each tunnel was a chalked Pokémon figure. As Maddy looked up and shone the light of her Goggles on the wall, Marco recognized one of them. "Hey, I think that's Grimer," he said, pointing to the blob-like Pokémon.

"Gross," said Maddy. "I don't like him."

"What?" said Marco. "I thought you never met a Pokémon you didn't like."

"Well, you're wrong," said Maddy, scrunching up her nose. "Grimer is slimy and stinky. I don't care if we find him or not."

Marco laughed out loud. "Maddy, the *poster* of Grimer won't be slimy or stinky. We have to try to find him. It's part of the game. C'mon." He led the way into the tunnel.

"I hope we find Zubat *first!*" said Maddy as she followed.

The tunnel was much narrower than the one they'd walked through before. Marco could stretch out his arms and touch both sides. Just a short ways in, he heard footsteps rushing toward him from behind. Before he could turn around and look, Maddy give a little *yelp*.

Then something slammed into Marco's back.

Hard.

CHAPTER TEN

Marco bounced off the wall as an enormous kid pushed past him.

"Hey, watch where you're going!" called Marco, rubbing his shoulder. He caught a glimpse of Max, the hulking Team Fennekin kid, barreling down the tunnel ahead.

Stella brushed by next, giving Maddy a sickly sweet smile. "Good luck finding Zubat," she said. "I'll bet there's a whole colony of bats in here, just waiting for you." She snickered and ran off after Max.

"I'm not even scared of bats!" Maddy called down the hall after Stella. Then she added, "Maybe Stella is, but I'm not!"

"I know you're not," said Marco. "Don't listen to her. Let's keep going."

A camera flash from the end of the tunnel told him that they were on the right track. Grimer, or some other Pokémon, was waiting for them down there. *But Team Fennekin is there, too,* Marco remembered. Then he heard footsteps running back down the tunnel toward them.

"If it's Stella, don't say anything to her," he whispered to Maddy. "Don't even look at her."

He couldn't help himself from looking at Max, though. The kid looked like a bull lumbering toward them. Marco stepped aside and flattened himself against the wall, pulling Maddy back with him.

Max jogged by without a word, but Stella made a face as she passed. She hissed her favorite line: "See ya, losers."

Marco didn't give her the satisfaction of reacting. Instead, he tugged on Maddy's hand and kept moving toward the cave.

"Eww," said Maddy. "Something stinks in there." She held her nose as they entered the small cave.

"Must be the trash can," said Marco. "What a weird place for one!"

He avoided it at first because of the smell. But after searching the cracks and crevices all around the cave, they still hadn't found a Pokémon. Then something caught Marco's eye—a Poké Ball dangling from the trash can.

"Look!" he said. A poster of Grimer was hanging on the back side of the can, almost out of view. "See, Maddy? He's not slimy at all."

"Well, he sure is stinky," said Maddy, who stayed on the other side of the room. "I told you he would be."

"You were right," said Marco, chuckling. "I wish we had our camera so we wouldn't have to come back here with Professor Birch and smell him all over again."

He expected Maddy to laugh at that. When she didn't, he straightened up to look for her. But the cave was totally empty.

"Maddy?"

His voice echoed off the walls and bounced right back to him, making the hair stand up on his arms.

"Maddy?" he called, louder this time. He hurried back toward the tunnel.

"Down here!" came a muffled response. Maddy was on her hands and knees on the floor of the tunnel.

When he saw her, he felt a wave of cool relief. "What are you doing?" he cried.

"Looking for Zubat!" she said happily. "See the picture? I told you Zubat would be here."

Marco scanned the wall looking for another Pokémon poster. What he saw instead was chalk art of a purplish bat. He reached out to touch it and felt the chalk smear beneath his fingers.

This art was different from the other art on the walls—brighter somehow. But it was definitely a Pokémon. And an arrow beneath Zubat pointed straight down.

Maddy's feet were now sticking out of the wall. She was crawling into some sort of tunnel. "Maddy!" Marco cried, squatting to get a better look.

The tunnel was a few feet high and the same distance wide. Maddy fit into it easily, but Marco wasn't so sure he wanted to follow.

"Don't go too far," he said. "You don't know where that leads."

But she was already gone, scurrying ahead of him like a speedy little mouse.

Marco's palms started to sweat. But he couldn't let Maddy crawl off into some weird tunnel all by herself. So he crouched down and started after her.

Tiny rocks dug into his knees as he crawled. His head kept brushing against the ceiling, which made him feel claustrophobic. As he bent his head and shoulders down lower, something dropped out of his pocket and clattered to the ground.

The compass!

Marco patted around in the dark with his hand, but he couldn't find it. "Maddy, I dropped the compass!" he called to her. "Bring back your Night Goggles!"

He could see a faint light from the tunnel ahead, but Maddy didn't respond. So he kept crawling after her in the darkness, with panic rising in his chest. "Maddy!" he called again.

Finally he caught up to her—his hand bumped against her sandal. "There you are!"

"That's the end," she said simply.

"What?"

"The tunnel ended. We have to go back."

Maddy sounded so matter of fact, but the panic in Marco's chest swelled. "I . . . I don't think I can turn around," he said.

"Crawl backwards, then!" Maddy said.

He tried—one knee scraping backwards, and then the other. He shut his eyes and focused on staying calm.

Maddy's sandals kept bumping into his hands. She was moving quickly, but he couldn't. *Left knee, right knee, left knee, right . . .* he chanted in his mind so that he wouldn't have to think about where he was or how much farther he had to go.

Then his knee hit something hard. Something painful. Something that *crunched* beneath him.

Marco knew with sick certainty exactly what it was.

"I found the compass," he said into the darkness, swallowing hard.

CHAPTER ELEVEN

Marco reached beneath his knee and pulled out the broken compass. He could feel the cracks in the plastic, but he tried not to think about them. *Just get out,* he told himself. He crawled backward as quickly as he could, until the tunnel brightened and cool air tickled his ankles. He'd made it—*finally.*

But the compass hadn't. As Marco rolled over and leaned against the wall, he studied it. The plastic cover was cracked and caved in, trapping the red arrow below.

Maddy popped out of the tunnel after him looking confused. "Where was Zubat?" she asked.

"Why'd the counselors draw that picture on the wall?"

Marco shook his head. "I don't know. But I busted the compass. We're going to need it for orienteering tomorrow, and I don't want to ask for another one from the counselors. They'll take away points for that, remember?"

The *thweet!* of Professor Birch's whistle drowned out Maddy's response.

Game over, thought Marco sadly.

There was no more time to search tunnels— little or big. They'd found only two of the four Pokémon. And not even a single glittery rock.

"Nisha!" Marco blinked into the bright sunlight, wondering if his eyes were playing tricks on him.

"Hey!" She rushed toward him and Maddy, looking much happier than Marco felt. "Did you find any Pokémon?"

"Just Grimer and Geodude," he said sadly. "We didn't have the camera, but we showed Professor Birch where we found them."

"I know—he told me," said Nisha. "I found the exact same ones. What are the chances of that?

But I also found some glittery rocks. So that's three points, right?"

"Did you find Zubat?" asked Maddy.

Nisha shot her a confused look. "Zubat isn't on the map." She pulled it from her pocket, just to be sure.

"But I saw Zubat's picture on the wall!" Maddy insisted. She told Nisha about the chalk drawing and the tunnel.

Marco shuddered, remembering the tight crawl through the claustrophobic tunnel.

"I'll bet anything Stella drew that picture of Zubat," said Nisha, lowering her voice.

"How do you know?" asked Maddy, spinning around to look for Stella.

Team Fennekin was whooping it up a few yards away—celebrating another victory as they got back onto their bikes.

"Two reasons," said Nisha. "First, Stella is a really good artist, remember?"

Marco remembered—he'd seen her sketchbook once, and she could draw Pokémon *really* well. He'd never tell her that though. She'd have to get a whole lot nicer first.

"What's the other reason?" asked Maddy.

Nisha's dark eyes flashed as she stole a look at Stella. "Didn't you see? She has purple chalk smeared all over her shorts."

Marco tried to catch a glimpse, but Stella was already pedaling away, leading her teammates down the road like a flock of obedient little birds. "We have to tell Professor Birch!" he said.

"Yeah," said Maddy. "That's cheating! And it made us lose points."

"We *could* tell him," said Nisha. "But we can't prove it was Stella."

"Besides," said Marco with a sigh, "we lost points for *lots* of reasons. Logan twisted his ankle so we were late, and then we forgot to get the camera from Logan, and then I . . . did this." He reluctantly held out the broken compass, showing Nisha his latest mistake.

For some reason, she didn't seem mad. "We can always get a new one from the counselors," she said, "but it'll cost us points. So *maybe* there's another way."

As she nibbled thoughtfully on a fingernail, Marco noticed she wasn't wearing gloves anymore. "What happened to your gloves?" he asked.

She glanced down in embarrassment. "Oh," she said, "I gave up on those. It was just too hard."

Maddy nodded, as if she knew just how Nisha felt.

Marco did, too. *Everything feels hard right now,* he thought. *And tomorrow is going to get a whole lot harder.*

Marco met the rest of Team Treecko at the Media Center after dinner. He was relieved to see Logan lying on the couch, playing Pokémon on a hand-held video game. His bandaged ankle rested on a Poké Ball cushion, and his crutches leaned against the end of the sofa.

"How does your ankle feel?" asked Marco. He hoped Logan would jump up and shout, "I'm healed! It's a miracle!" Maybe he'd even do a little dance. *That* was the friend Marco knew and loved.

But Logan barely glanced his way. "Okay," he mumbled. "Still sore."

Maddy sat beside him in an overstuffed chair. "Do you want to hold Dedenne?" she asked, holding out a shoebox. Her little brown mouse was nibbling on lettuce, casting wary glances up at Logan. "Dedenne's leg was hurt when we found him, remember? But it got better. Yours will get better, too."

"I can't hold him right now," said Logan, waving the video game in his hand. "I'm playing Pokémon. Professor Sycamore showed me how to go down deeper in Granite Cave."

"Professor Sycamore is here?" asked Maddy, searching the room for her favorite counselor.

He ran a kitchen "lab" where kids could make Poké Puffs, and Maddy had practically lived there the first week of camp. When she spotted him in his white lab coat across the room, she waved.

Marco waited for Logan to ask how things went at the cave, but he never did. *Doesn't he even care?* wondered Marco. So finally, he just told him— about the forgotten camera, the fake drawing of Zubat, and the chalk on Stella's shorts.

Logan's face clouded with emotion. "It's my fault," he said. "If I hadn't hurt my ankle, I would have been there with the camera."

"No!" said Marco. "I made lots of mistakes, too." He wished someone—Maddy or even Logan maybe—would speak up and say that he *hadn't*, but neither of them did.

"Hey, do you want to hear a joke?" asked Maddy brightly. "I just made up a good one. Which Pokémon is really good at baseball?"

When no one answered, she declared, "Zu-BAT! Get it?"

Marco grinned. "That's actually pretty good," he said.

But Logan grimaced. "Enough about bats," he said. "Can we talk about something else?"

So much for laughter being the best medicine, thought Marco. He was starting to feel sick to his stomach.

"Shh! Listen up!" Nisha rushed over and took a seat on the floor next to Maddy's chair. "Professor Sycamore is about to show team scores for Pokémon Orienteering. Watch the screen!"

The Pokémon movie paused, and Professor Sycamore's voice came over the loudspeaker. "Good evening, Orienteers! After a full day of hiking, canoeing, and cave exploring, we thought you might want to see exactly how your team stacks up in this weekend's Pokémon Orienteering challenge. Are we ready?"

Cheers and murmurs swelled from around the room, but Marco stared down at his hands. He was afraid to look.

When he heard Maddy squeal, he finally glanced up. And there it was in black and white—the top three teams:

```
TEAM FENNEKIN: 14
TEAM TORCHIC:  12
TEAM TREECKO:  10
```

"Third place?" said Logan, slapping his good leg. "That stinks!"

"It's better than fourth or fifth," Maddy said sweetly, stroking Dedenne's head.

"But there's more!" boomed Professor Sycamore's voice. "Tomorrow is our last day of orienteering, and it will take us to the lovely and mystical Crescent Isle. There, you'll search for a single Pokémon: the legendary Cresselia."

The movie screen filled with color, and there was the legendary Pokémon.

"Cresselia!" Maddy lifted Dedenne out of his box so that he could see, too.

Cresselia looked like something out of a fairy tale—a blue, swan-like Pokémon with a majestic yellow head and pink ring-like wings. Marco wanted to *ooh* and *ahh* over the Pokémon like everyone else. But right now, he didn't care if he *ever* found Cresselia. *Because the only way to capture that Pokémon is to cross the zip line*, he thought with a shudder.

Then Professor Sycamore said something that set the room abuzz. "Because Cresselia is the last Pokémon to capture, and because the journey to Crescent Isle will be the most challenging, Cresselia will be worth *more* points than any other Pokémon."

Marco's ears pricked. *How many points?*

"If you're lucky enough to spot Cresselia on Crescent Isle, your team will be awarded *five* points," Professor Sycamore announced dramatically.

"Five?" Logan sat straight up.

Nisha's eyes widened.

And Maddy nearly dropped Dedenne, who squeaked and tried to run up her sleeve.

Logan sucked in his breath. "You're so lucky that you get to ride the zip line," he said to Marco. "You could be the one who finds Cresselia and puts Team Treecko back on top! I'd change places with you in a *second*."

Nisha laughed out loud. "But Marco doesn't even *want* to ride the zip line!" she blurted.

"What?" Logan said.

As their words rang in Marco's head, his body started to tingle. His cheeks burned. *How did Nisha know?* he wondered. *How could she?*

Everyone was staring at him—he could *feel* it. They were waiting for him to say something, to tell Nisha she was wrong.

But she wasn't.

And right now, Marco wished he were a mouse like Dedenne—so he could crawl into a hole and never come out.

CHAPTER TWELVE

"I'm sorry, Marco," Nisha said quickly, clamping her hand over her mouth. "I shouldn't have said that. I found your letter in your trashcan, but I shouldn't have said anything."

"Wait, you were digging through our trash?" asked Logan.

"I was looking for more 3-D goggles!" Nisha explained. "I thought I could make a pair of glasses for each of us. But I found Marco's letter to his parents instead."

"What did it say?" asked Maddy.

Nisha shook her head. "I'm sorry, Marco," she said, her eyes rimmed with guilt. "Please don't be mad."

Marco tried to swallow the Shroomish in his throat. He wasn't mad exactly. Just scared, as usual. Scared that his friends would think he was a big baby if they knew the truth.

But now he had no choice. He had to tell them.

"I'm afraid to ride the zip line."

The words sounded tinny and far away, as if someone else had said them. And the silence that followed seemed like an eternity. Marco kept talking, just to fill it. But he kept his eyes on the floor.

"I didn't want you guys to know how scared I was. Because you're all so brave—you're not scared of anything."

When Marco finally glanced up at his friends, Maddy was smiling.

"That's dumb," she said.

"What?" Marco almost laughed out loud. "Why is it dumb?"

"It's dumb because *everybody* is scared of *something*." Maddy hesitated and then said, "I'm scared of the water. Because I don't know how to swim."

This time, everyone whirled around to face Maddy.

"Really?" said Nisha. "Is that why you wouldn't go in the canoe?"

Maddy nodded as she stroked Dedenne's head.

Marco felt something warm spread through his insides. "Thanks for telling me, Maddy," he said. "That was pretty brave."

Hearing Maddy's confession *did* make him feel better. *But still,* he thought, *she's younger than me. She's supposed to be scared of more things.*

And Logan was being awfully quiet. *Does he think I'm a loser?* Marco wondered.

"Everybody's scared of something," Maddy repeated.

"Not Logan," Marco couldn't help arguing.

But his friend surprised him by sitting up on the couch. "That's not exactly true."

"He's scared of bats," said Maddy matter-of-factly.

"No, he's not!" said Marco. "He thought the bat at the cave was funny. Right?"

But Logan wouldn't look at him. And that's when Marco knew the truth: Logan *was* scared of bats. He really was!

"So . . . did you hurt your ankle for real?" asked Nisha slowly, as if choosing her words carefully. "Or were you just afraid to go inside the cave today?"

Logan's cheeks turned crimson. "Both. I mean I *did* hurt my ankle, but . . . maybe it's not that bad." He rotated his foot in a small circle.

"So you can do the zip line!" said Marco, jumping up.

Logan shook his head sadly. "No. Nurse Joy and Professor Birch talked, and they won't let me."

Disappointment washed over Marco all over again.

"What are *you* scared of, Nisha?" asked Maddy.

"I don't know—let me think about that," answered Nisha, nibbling on a nail.

"Maybe she's scared that one day, she'll chew her fingers right off!" joked Logan. He seemed relieved that the spotlight was on someone else now.

"Hey! Not funny," said Nisha, swatting his arm.

"Sorry," said Logan, sinking back in his seat. "Joking helps me feel less nervous about things."

Really? thought Marco. *Is that why Logan jokes around so much?*

"I get that," Nisha said thoughtfully, then turned back to Maddy. "What I *really* worry about is that one of my inventions won't work. That it'll be a total disaster and I'll let you all down."

"Really?" said Marco. "That's what you're scared of? But that's never happened. Your inventions always work great!"

Nisha shrugged. "It could happen."

Just like the zip line could fail, thought Marco, nodding. *It could happen.* He tried to chase the thought away by focusing on the positives. "At least there are still three of us doing the zip line tomorrow. So if I chicken out, you and Maddy have my back, right?"

"Of course!" said Nisha.

But Maddy fell quiet. When her cheeks got blotchy, Marco's heart began to *thud* in his ears.

"Maddy," he said. "You're doing the zip line, right?"

She shook her head. "It goes over water," she said, her voice trembling. "And I don't like water, remember?"

Marco sank back against the couch pillow, wrapping his arms tightly around his body. He wanted to be mad. How could Maddy do this to him? But he knew how she could—and why. Maddy was just as scared of water as he was of heights.

Nisha gave him a reassuring smile. "So it's you and me on the zip line," she said. "Do you think you can do it?"

Marco shrugged. He wiped his sweaty palms on his shorts and told his friends the honest truth. "I don't know."

Then he caught Logan's eye and said, "You'd better make sure my harness is really tight, because I'm probably going to faint." He was kidding, sort of. And when Logan laughed, Marco felt a hint of pride. Cracking a joke helped—at least a little.

"Alright," said Nisha. "I have to go. I have *one* more invention to make tonight, and it had better work!"

Marco's other teammates began leaving, too, one by one.

"I'm going to spy on Nisha," said Maddy, holding a finger to her lips. "I'll report back on her big invention in the morning." She put the lid on Dedenne's box and hurried toward the door.

Then Logan reached for his crutches. "Professor Sycamore is going to teach me about Super Training my Pokémon. Wanna come?"

Marco shook his head. "No," he said. "I have to finish my Wingull letter." He didn't know what made him say that, or even if he'd do it. The words just popped out of his mouth.

"Okay," said Logan. "But make sure it doesn't end up in the trash. You never know who might read it!" He grinned and hobbled toward the other end of the Media Center.

And then Marco was alone again.

And his fears began to creep back in.

Don't think about the zip line, he told himself. But he *had* to think about it. He was running out of time!

Tomorrow is the big day, thought Marco, his throat tightening. *And when that whistle blows, there's no turning back.*

CHAPTER THIRTEEN

"**K**nock, knock."

"Who's there?" mumbled Marco, still half asleep.

"Zubat," said the voice. Where was it coming from?

"Zubat who?" asked Marco.

"Zu-batter wake up. It's zip line time!"

Marco sat up with a start, and heard Logan laughing from his bed across the room. He fought the urge to whip a pillow at him for making such bad jokes.

Today's no joke, Marco remembered. *It's zip line day. Ready or not.*

It helped, though, that Logan was back to his usual jokey self.

"Hey, Marco," he said as they walked to breakfast. "Why are Zubats hard to get along with?"

"I don't know," said Marco. "Why?"

"Because they can be a real pain in the neck!" said Logan, doing his best vampire impersonation. Then he started right in on the next one. "Which Pokémon likes to visit animals?"

Marco grinned. "Let me guess. A ZOO-bat?"

"Yes!" Logan threw back his head and laughed hysterically.

This could go on all day, thought Marco. But he was glad his friend was back to normal. As they headed to breakfast together, Marco *almost* felt hungry, in spite of the butterflies fluttering inside him.

Just outside the Dining Hall, they met Maddy running toward them from the girls' cabins. Her cheeks were flushed, and she looked like she was bursting with a huge secret.

She held out her closed fist in front of Marco. Then she opened it to reveal a woven bracelet made of pink, orange, and white floss. "For you," she said. "A Focus Band. I made it."

"A Focus Band?" he asked.

"Yeah," she said. "You know—they keep Pokémon from fainting during attacks. So now you won't faint on the zip line." She said it with such certainty that Marco almost believed her.

"You know, Maddy," said Logan in his I-can't-resist-messing-with-you voice, "Focus Bands aren't actually *real.*"

She blew her bangs off her forehead and stared at him for a long, hard moment. "I *know* that, Logan," she finally said. "I'm not a little kid. But I'm trying to help Marco. And sometimes it's good to pretend."

"She's got a point," said Marco. "Thanks, Maddy!"

"Wait till you see what Nisha made, too," she said, bouncing up and down. She was obviously *dying* to tell them about Nisha's invention, but she didn't.

Before heading into the Dining Hall, Marco remembered something he had to do. "I'll catch up with you," he told his friends. "I've got to go mail a Wingull letter."

He'd written it late last night, when he couldn't sleep. And this time, he hadn't even thought about what he was writing—he'd just told his parents the truth. He talked about the zip line, and about how scared he was, and about how good he would feel when it was all over.

After dropping the letter in the Wingull mailbox, he felt even better. Lighter somehow. But as he turned away, something caught his eye. *A feather?*

He bent down to pick it up. The soft blue feather was enormous—it stretched from his elbow almost to his fingertips. *That's a big bird,* he thought, *and a pretty one.*

He stuck the feather partway into his pocket and hurried back toward the Dining Hall, hoping he'd be able to eat.

"It's a Cresselia feather!" Maddy insisted as they walked toward the zip line after breakfast. "It's big and blue. What other kind of bird could that come from?"

"Well, he found it by the Wingull box. So I'm going out on a limb here and guessing a Wingull, maybe?" joked Logan. He was using just one crutch now and moving a whole lot faster.

"No, it's from a Cresselia," Maddy insisted. "And holding a Cresselia feather cures you from nightmares."

"Really?" said Marco, running his finger along the soft edges of the feather. "Will it cure me from *daymares,* too? Because in about fifteen minutes, I'm about to have one."

"Yes," said Maddy. "It will." Her eyes twinkled.

It's fun to pretend for a while, Marco decided. Right now, he was pretending he was walking to school. Or to a friend's house. *Anywhere* but to the zip line. He hoped Maddy would keep chatting so that he wouldn't have to face reality just yet.

But after they'd passed the girls' cabins and the pier, there was no more pretending. The zip line towered over Marco like a Mega Steelix, taller than he remembered. It cast a dark shadow on the lake beyond.

Marco's fingers found the Focus Band on his wrist, and he spun it around and around. *At least I won't faint,* he thought with a smile. But the ground beneath him felt kind of wobbly, and he decided to sit down to wait for Nisha.

Every time he heard voices, he turned, hoping to see Nisha's face. Most of the teams were here, and Professor Birch was already handing out orienteering maps. But still, no Nisha. Where *was* she?

Logan seemed antsy, too. He held his crutch like a rifle, pretending to scope out ducks on the lake—or maybe wild Pokémon. Marco didn't ask which. He was too busy wondering what he was going to do if Nisha didn't show up.

If she doesn't come, he realized with a sickening feeling, *I'll* have *to do the zip line. I won't have a choice!*

He glanced back at the woods, wondering if he should make a run for it now. And then he saw her. *Nisha!*

She jogged toward him like a superhero—or a girl who could turn into one at any moment.

"Where's your invention?" asked Maddy, jumping up from the grass. "Show Marco!"

"Just wait," said Nisha, raising a finger in the air. But her eyes flashed the way they always did when she'd created something good—*really* good. "Marco, can you run down the list of things we need?"

"Um, sure," he said.

But just then, Professor Birch hurried past. "Good morning, Team Treecko," he said in his sing-songy voice. "Nice to see you here early, and all together." He chuckled as he handed Nisha a crisp orienteering map. Then he headed for the zip line tower, his whistle bouncing against his clipboard as he walked.

"Okay," said Marco. "So we have the map."

"Check," said Nisha, grinning.

"Camera?"

"Check," said Logan. He dug Dex out of his pocket and handed it to Marco.

"Stopwatch?" said Marco. He smiled and pointed at the lanyard around his neck. "Check." Running down the checklist helped him stay calm. He was glad Nisha had asked him to do it.

"Anything else?" asked Nisha, tapping her foot impatiently.

But Marco couldn't think. He ran a hand over his head, trying to remember.

"Compass!" Maddy answered for him. "Duh."

"Oh, yeah." Marco's face fell. He could still hear the *crunch* of the compass beneath his knee in that dark tunnel. "We don't actually have one of those, thanks to me."

"*Actually,*" Nisha corrected him, "we do." She reached for her backpack. Out of the mesh side pocket, she pulled out what looked like a travel mug.

"Hot chocolate?" asked Logan hopefully.

"No!" said Maddy. "It's the compass!"

"Really?" Marco moved in for a closer look.

When Nisha popped off the lid, he saw that the mug was halfway filled with water. And something floated on the surface—a circle cut out of cork, with a needle sticking through it.

"It points north," Nisha announced proudly. "I rubbed the needle over a strong magnet to magnetize it."

"That's *really* cool," said Marco, leaning over the mug.

"*Cooler* than hot chocolate," said Logan. "Get it?" He cracked up at his own joke.

Marco laughed, too, but then he caught the look on Nisha's face. She was staring up at the sun. "Wait a minute," she said slowly. "The needle *isn't* pointing north. North is *that* way." She gestured toward the woods.

Marco looked at the needle again, which was pointing in the exact opposite direction—toward the boathouse on the lake. "Right," he said. "It's pointing . . . south."

"Oh, no," whimpered Nisha. "No, no, no, no, no. It was working last night. I must have set it down by another magnet. Or something made of iron. Or something in my backpack. . . ." She crouched down and started frantically digging through her backpack, looking for the culprit.

When she came up empty-handed, she turned to Marco with wild eyes. She looked like she was going to throw up.

It's her worst fear! he suddenly realized. *One of her inventions didn't work.*

"It's okay," he said quickly. "We can get another compass from the counselors, remember? It's no big deal." He wasn't sure that there was time, and they'd lose a point or two if they had to ask for a new one. But it didn't matter. He just wanted Nisha to feel better.

"Yeah, it's okay, Nisha," said Maddy, patting her shoulder.

Nisha squeezed her eyes shut for what felt like a long time. When she opened them again, the old Nisha was back. "Okay. I'll go ask Professor Birch if he has a compass." She sprang up from the ground and ran toward the tower.

But seconds later, she was back, shaking her head. "We have to get one at the Media Center," she said. "And it'll cost us a point."

"We don't need it," Marco said quickly.

"Yes, we do!" Nisha insisted. "Cresselia is going to be tough to find without a compass. And we *need* to capture Cresselia *and* the hidden item to win this game!"

When Professor Birch blew his whistle from the top of the zip line tower, Nisha sprang into action. "I'm going to the Media Center. I'll sprint the whole way. You take the zip line to the island, and I'll meet you there."

She pressed the map into Marco's hand, and then she was gone—before he could say a word.

Loneliness washed over him, and a ringing sound filled his ears. Maddy was saying something, but he couldn't hear a word of it. Because Maddy wasn't going on the zip line. Logan wasn't either. And Nisha was running in the opposite direction, like a compass needle gone awry.

I'm on my own, Marco realized. *Nisha's worst fear came true. And mine just did, too.*

CHAPTER FOURTEEN

Another whistle blew. Professor Birch said something into a megaphone, but the words jumbled together in Marco's ears. And then Logan was pushing him forward toward the steps of the zip line.

Marco's legs moved, but he didn't feel like he was controlling them. He couldn't control *any* of this. It felt like a bad dream, rolling forward all on its own.

A line was forming—one kid from each team. Marco fell in behind a fox-orange shirt. And then he was climbing.

When a cool breeze hit his face, he felt himself slowly waking up.

I'm on my own, he thought again. No Maddy, with her big imagination. No Logan, telling jokes to distract him. And no Nisha, with her clever inventions.

He could still picture Nisha's face—how she looked when she realized the compass was broken. *Like the sky was going to fall,* he remembered. *Except it didn't.*

He remembered how everyone had gathered around Nisha to tell her it was okay. And how she had somehow pulled herself up and kept going.

She faced her fears, thought Marco. *I really hope I can too.*

As he reached for the railing of the steps, something tickled his hand. He glanced down to see the big blue feather sticking out of his pocket, just behind the folded map.

I don't have my friends, he thought, *but I have a Cresselia feather.*

"And your Focus Band!" he could almost hear Maddy saying.

So he clung tight to both and kept climbing.

"Just get up there, you big baby!"

The orange T-shirt in front of Marco wasn't budging. Sam was glued to the stairs, with Stella hollering at him from down below.

"What's wrong?" asked Marco.

Sam whirled around. "My legs won't move," he whispered. His freckled face was flushed with fear.

Marco hesitated for just a second before telling Sam the truth. "I know," he said. "I'm scared too." It felt good to say the words out loud again, even to a member of Team Fennekin. *I sure hope he doesn't use them against me someday,* thought Marco. But the terrified look on Sam's face made Marco think he probably wouldn't.

"Do you want me to go first?" he asked. The words flew out of his mouth, and he instantly wished he could stuff them back in. *Say no, say no, say no.*

But Sam nodded.

Ugh. Marco took a deep breath, carefully passed Sam on the staircase, and climbed the last row of stairs to reach Professor Birch.

"Ah, Team Treecko," said Professor Birch good-naturedly. "You'll be the first team on the island today."

Marco couldn't respond. He'd just made the mistake of looking down over the rail. The ground was a *long* ways away. And the zip line tower across the water? Even farther away. Officer Jenny was a speck of white and blue, ready to greet anyone who survived the journey. She waved to Marco, but he couldn't let go of the railing long enough to wave back.

"Let's get you harnessed in," said Professor Birch.

With buckles and straps around his chest, waist, and legs, Marco felt like he was wearing a straight jacket. His heart began *thump, thump, thump*ing in his ears.

"Do you want me to hold your feather?" asked Professor Birch. "You don't want to lose that—it's a beauty. Could be from a great blue heron."

"Huh?" Marco looked down and saw that he was clutching the feather for dear life. "Um, no. I'm good."

"Alright," said Professor Birch. "Then I'll just release the tether here." He explained what he was doing step by step, maybe because Marco had already scrunched his eyes shut.

As he felt the ground drop out from beneath him, he heard someone scream from far away. *Is that me?* he wondered with horror, clamping his mouth shut.

To fight the fear, he imagined his friends beside him—Maddy on his left and Logan on his right.

He could picture Logan cracking jokes, one after the other. He felt himself slowly start to relax.

But wait, where was Nisha in this fantasy? *Right behind us,* Marco decided. *She's probably flying on something she invented herself.*

He imagined his Focus Band glowing pink and orange, giving him strength. And the feather in his hand *was* from Cresselia—he knew for certain that it was. In fact, he imagined himself riding on the Pokémon's back, its ring-like wings rising and falling with a magical rhythm. He could feel the cool wind on his face as Cresselia soared toward Crescent Isle.

Then suddenly, someone was calling his name. Marco fought to open his eyes, as if he'd been in a deep sleep. And there was Officer Jenny in front of him—waving from the platform on the island.

His harness hit something in the wire above, and after a *bump, bump, bump,* he slowed to a stop.

"Well, how was it?" asked Officer Jenny as she helped unbuckle his harness.

Marco couldn't speak. But as he started down the steps on his wobbly legs, he couldn't stop smiling.

When he found his footing, Marco started to explore the island. It was green and wooded, like much of Camp Pikachu. But for a moment, he couldn't remember what he was looking for. Pokémon? Which ones?

The feather in his hand reminded him: *Cresselia*. There would be just one Pokémon to find here on Crescent Isle.

But for some reason, Marco wasn't in a hurry to find it. He didn't have a compass, at least not until Nisha got here.

He listened to the shrieks and squeals of other campers crossing the zip line, and knew that soon the island would be crawling with kids. But for now, he felt like the first man on the moon.

He walked along the edge of the island, away from the zip line toward a quiet, marshlike area. With each step, his feet sunk a little into the earth. *Squish, squish, squish.* Cool water seeped into one shoe, but Marco didn't care.

It felt so quiet here, almost dreamlike. And then he saw it—a tall, majestic bird with a pinkish chest and deep blue feathers. It stood perfectly still at the water's edge just a few yards away.

As Marco held his breath and watched, the bird turned its head slowly, as if to say hello. It took a few slow, graceful steps with its stork-like legs.

And then, without warning, it crouched low and sprang into the air. Giant wings flapped and lifted the bird out of the water.

Marco shaded his eyes to watch the beautiful bird circle the marsh and then disappear into the morning sun.

"Marco!"

He turned back expecting to see Nisha rushing toward him. But it wasn't Nisha at all. Maddy's blonde pigtails bounced up and down as she ran along the wet ground.

"You did the zip line?" he said. "But I thought you were scared of the water!"

Maddy shrugged. "You were scared too," she said. "But you did it anyway. And I didn't want you to be by yourself. So I just closed my eyes and pretended I was flying over grass."

Marco laughed. "I pretended on the way over, too," he confessed. "Hey, did you see that bird that just flew away?"

She nodded. "Was it Cresselia?" she asked, her eyes twinkling.

He cocked his head and smiled. "I think it *could* have been."

A crowd of kids hurried past, including Sam and Stella. They had their camera out, ready to be the first to capture a Pokémon. But Sam slowed down just enough to smile at Marco.

"Hey," Marco heard Stella say as she passed. "They found the hidden item!"

Marco and Maddy looked at each other. "Did we?" Maddy asked.

Marco slid the map out of his pocket, careful not to disturb the Cresselia feather. And sure enough, the hidden item marked on Crescent Isle was *feathers*.

"We found the hidden item!" said Maddy. "And we already saw Cresselia too, right?"

"I think so," said Marco. "We don't have a picture to prove it yet, but we have something even better."

He grinned as he handed her the feather. Then he held out the map in front of him, ready to lead the way.